Josh Taylor,
Mr. Average

Three kids, one friendship, and a bunch of crazy adventures!

#1 *Here's Hilary!*

#2 *Josh Taylor, Mr. Average*

Coming soon:
#3 *Hilary's Super Secret*

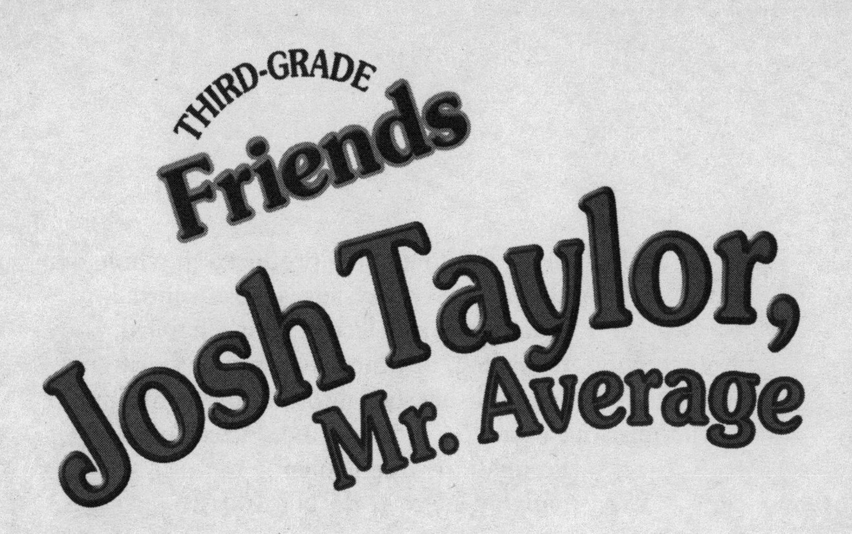

by Suzanne Williams

Illustrated by George Ulrich

A
LITTLE APPLE
PAPERBACK

SCHOLASTIC INC.
New York Toronto London Auckland Sydney
Mexico City New Delhi Hong Kong Buenos Aires

ISBN 0-439-32989-2

12 11 10 9 8 7 6 5 4 3 2 3 4 5 6 7/0

Printed in the U.S.A. 40
First printing, November 2002

To Jane Gardner, Phyllis Anderson, Susan Nickel, and all the other wonderful librarians I've worked with, or had the pleasure to meet, over the years.

Contents

1
Stuck in the Middle

"Hey, everyone, I'm home!" I called out as I walked in the door from school. Mom waved from the living room couch. She was busy reading a book to my little sister, Angie. As usual, I was starved. I dropped my backpack in the hall, then headed for the kitchen to paw through the cupboards to look for a snack. The phone rang, and my older brother,

Brock, sprinted into the room. "I've got it, Josh!" he yelled at me.

"Fine," I said, pulling down a box of granola bars. Most phone calls are for him anyway. The callers are usually girls. I suppose they think Brock's good-looking just because he's tall and lean, with wavy brown hair. Luckily for him, he didn't inherit Dad's big ears. Mine stick out from my head "like two big mushrooms," my friend Hilary says. I can wiggle them without even touching them.

I sat down at the kitchen table and opened the box of granola bars. Brock sat across from me with the phone. From the soft way he was speaking, I guessed I'd been right about there being a girl on the other end of the line. I wouldn't *want* girls calling me — except Hilary. Because she's not a *girl* girl. We've been friends since first grade, and she's the best wall-ball player in our third-grade classroom. I used to be second-best, but now I'm third-best.

I unwrapped a granola bar and took a bite. Besides being better-looking than me, my brother's a straight-A student and a star on the high school varsity swim team — the only ninth grader on the team. *I* mostly get average grades, and I'm not a good swimmer at all. I had to take the beginner's class *three times* before I passed. Whenever I tried to float, I sank like a rock. When I complained that I'd never be able to swim as well as Brock, my swimming instructor said, "That's okay, Josh. Just do it for the exercise. Swimming is good exercise." Well, if swimming is such good exercise, I wanted to ask him, why are whales so fat?

My little sister, Angie, who is only four, wandered into the room. "I want one!" she shouted when she saw me eating a granola bar.

Brock frowned, putting his finger to his mouth to shush her.

Angie scowled at him. She hates it when he does that. She and Brock don't get along very well, to tell you the truth. Brock doesn't know how to handle her. Angie'll do almost anything you ask if you just pay attention to her and joke around with her a bit.

I stripped the wrapper off another granola bar and handed it to Angie.

She smiled at me. "Thanks, Josh."

"Hey, Angie," I said, keeping my voice low so as not to disturb Brock. "Why did the chicken cross the playground?" It was a joke I learned from my other best friend, Gordon. He and I used to be enemies, but that was before I really got to know him. Now he and Hilary and I are all friends.

Angie cocked her head. "To get to the other side?"

"No," I said. "To get to the other *slide*."

Angie giggled, and her blond curls bounced. She has long eyelashes, too. Grown-ups are always saying how "cute" she is, and it's true. Luckily, she didn't get dad's ears, either.

Angie eyed the granola bar box. Suddenly, she stabbed a finger at a word on the box. "Ch-ch-ch. What's this say, Josh?"

I looked at the box. "Chewy," I told her.

Angie studied the picture on the box and pointed to two other words. "Chocolate chip," she said proudly. "This says 'chocolate chip'."

"That's right," I told her. "Good for you."

Like I said, Angie's only four. But already she's reading. *I* didn't start reading till

Granola
Bars
CHEWY
CHOCOLATE CHI

first grade. And it took me a long time to get so I didn't have to sound out every word.

My mom and dad say Angie's "precocious." I looked up the word in my dictionary — once I finally figured out how to spell it. It means "early mental development." In other words, she's *smart*. Just like Brock. But me? I'm stuck in the middle. Average smarts. Average looks. And except for wall-ball, average at sports, too. I'm so average, in fact, that sometimes I think I might as well be *invisible.*

2
Mr. Average

At school the next day, I could hardly wait for morning recess so I could play wall-ball. Like I said, compared to other sports I'm not too bad at wall-ball. I may be only third-best now that Gordon's learned to play, but at least that's not average. And I don't *really* mind that Gordon's better than me — now that we're friends.

During reading, I sneaked up to Hilary's

desk toward the front of the room. "Prepare to meet your doom," I hissed. "I'm going to beat you at wall-ball this morning."

Hilary laughed. "Fat chance. Who do you think you're kidding?"

I wiggled my ears. "I don't know. What's your name?"

As Hilary stifled a giggle, Ms. Foster, our teacher, glanced up from her desk and frowned. "I better go," I whispered. I crept to my desk at the back of the room.

When the recess bell rang, I grabbed a yellow rubber ball and ran outside to the wall-ball courts. Hilary and Gordon joined me just a minute later. We played rock, paper, scissors to decide who would serve first, and Gordon won.

"Eggs-cellent," he said, taking his place on the court. "I can just see the headlines. 'CHICKEN BOY SCRAMBLES OPPONENTS!'"

Hilary and I groaned. Hilary nicknamed Gordon "Chicken Boy" because he used to make *tsk-tsk* noises all the time, like a chicken pecking seeds. Plus he's afraid of doing anything that might get him into trouble. The nickname was an *insult*. How were we supposed to know Gordon would decide he *liked* his nickname and want to keep it? Now we have to put up with a lot of bad chicken jokes.

Hilary stepped up to play Gordon first. A line of about ten other kids quickly formed behind us. Gordon threw the ball in the air. "Double!" he shouted. The ball bounced before Gordon struck it with both hands clasped together. Hitting the ground again, the ball flew up to meet the wall just above the service line. Hilary ran left to catch it on the rebound.

She smacked the ball hard. It hit the

ground then spun sideways, bouncing low against the wall before dropping to Gordon's right. Gordon had to run up close to make the return; the ball almost bounced twice. His return was weak, and Hilary was waiting for it. She finished him off with a hard smack that sent the ball deep into the court behind him.

"New headline," I whispered to Gordon as I stepped up to take his place. "Opponent Eggs-ecutes Chicken Boy." I drew a finger across my throat.

Gordon laughed. He and Hilary and I are always teasing one another like that. "May *your* fortune be superior to mine," he said. Anybody else would've said "I hope you have better luck," but that's just the way Gordon talks sometimes. You get used to it after a while.

My fortune wasn't superior, though. In

fact, I didn't even return Hilary's first serve — which should've been an easy one since it landed right in the middle of the court. When I swung to hit the ball, I missed it completely. "Aww, man," I said. "I've *never* played *this* badly before."

Hilary grinned. "You mean you've played this game before? That *is* hard to believe."

If it was my *first* game, at least I'd have an excuse, I thought, disgusted with myself. "Oh, well," I muttered as I headed for the end of the line. "At least I'm a good example of what *not* to do."

Third best at wall-ball? Ha! I sighed, feeling even more average than ever.

After recess, Ms. Foster passed back the spelling tests we'd taken earlier in the morning. Her dark hair frizzed around her head like a rain cloud as she reached out to hand me mine.

Later, while she was writing something on the blackboard, Gordon and Hilary and I compared scores. Gordon got his usual one hundred percent, and Hilary only missed one word. Guess who missed four? That's right. Josh Taylor. *Mr. Average.*

In the middle of math, the door opened and a couple of older kids from another class — a boy and a girl — came into our room. They crossed to Ms. Foster's desk and spoke with her a few seconds. It was too noisy to hear what they were saying. A moment later, Ms. Foster clapped her hands to get our attention. "Boys and girls," she said, "We have visitors. This is Cindy Blair and Tony Smith from Ms. Thompson's fifth-grade class."

The kids smiled at us, and Tony, a tall, thin boy with glasses, even waved.

"Cindy and Tony have come to tell us

about a very important decision we need to make by the end of the week," said Ms. Foster. "Please give them your undivided attention."

The room quieted as we all stared at Cindy and Tony, waiting to hear what they were going to say.

They glanced at each other. "You start," said Tony.

"Okay," said Cindy. She tossed her head, and her long black ponytail swung from side to side. "We're here to speak to you about Student Council," she said.

I knew about Student Council. They're a group of kids chosen from every classroom except the youngest grades. They meet a couple of times every month to come up with ideas and make decisions about things that concern the whole school.

"Student Council has planned and carried out a lot of important projects," Cindy was saying. "Last year, we organized a canned food drive and we also collected used books for kids in a homeless shelter."

I remembered the food drive. I'd brought a huge bag from home filled with boxes of macaroni and cheese, and cans of stuff like green beans, corn, tuna fish, and chili. Mom had tried to get me to take a can of split-pea soup that had been in our cupboard a long time because no one wanted to eat it. "Why should poor people have to eat something we wouldn't eat?" I asked her. She didn't have an answer for that.

Now Tony spoke up. "Student Council does 'just-for-fun' stuff, too. Last year, we planned two all-school parties and School Spirit Days like Funny Hat Day and Wear Your Clothes Backward Day."

I remembered those things, too. On Funny

Hat Day, I'd worn my pillow to school, tied around my head with a belt. My "hat" got a lot of laughs, but it wasn't very comfortable.

Cindy spoke again. "We're here to ask you to choose the best person to represent your class on the council. We'll be announcing the names of all the representatives to the whole school at the end of the day on Thursday."

After Cindy and Tony left, Ms. Foster

said we would vote to decide on our representative during social studies on Thursday. She said that we would talk some more about the election tomorrow, on Wednesday, and see who'd be interested in the job.

I thought about how cool it would be to represent our class on the Student Council. But I was *Mr. Average.* Why would anyone choose *me* for an important job like that?

3
The Secret Tapes

As we went back to our math lesson, I sneaked peeks at everyone in the classroom. I thought about the things each person was good at. Carl, who sits next to me, is a whiz at science. In second grade, he brought a chemistry set to school for Show and Tell. He wanted to show our class how to make a stink bomb, but the teacher wouldn't let him.

The best artist in our class is Alicia Garcia. Her favorite thing to draw is cats. She's crazy about them. Hilary is best at wall-ball, of course, and Gordon is best at just about every school subject there is: math, spelling, reading, social studies — every single one of them.

I scratched out a wrong answer on my math worksheet and chewed on my pencil. If only *I* could be best at something, too.

It was almost time for lunch when the door to our classroom opened. A dark-haired woman came into our room, carrying a large silver tray of pink-frosted cupcakes. Alicia hopped up and ran over to her. Then I remembered that today was Alicia's birthday. Her mom had brought treats for the class.

Mrs. Garcia said something to Alicia that I couldn't understand. Then Alicia said something back, and I realized they weren't speaking English at all. They were speaking Spanish. Wow! It sounded so cool. No one in *my* family speaks another language. And that's when I came up with this great plan. *I'd* learn to speak a language, but a different one than Alicia. Then I could be best at something, too!

After lunch, I asked Ms. Foster if I could go to the library during recess.

Ms. Foster looked surprised. She probably wondered why I'd want to go to the library during recess when recess is my favorite part of the day. "Library Day is tomorrow," she said. "Do you want to wait till then?"

"Not really," I said. I wanted to get started on my plan right away.

"Okay. Fine." Ms. Foster handed me a library pass.

When the recess bell rang, I told Hilary and Gordon I'd have to miss playing wall-ball.

"Why?" they asked at the same time.

I wiggled my ears. "It's a secret."

Hilary rolled her eyes. "If it's a *secret*," she said, "everyone in the world will know about it soon."

"Ha-ha," I said. But it's true, I have a hard time keeping secrets.

"We're your friends," Gordon said. "You can tell *us*."

I sighed. "It's nothing really. I have to go to the library, that's all." I wasn't sure I wanted them to know about my plan to learn a language. Not yet, anyway. Not until I got really good at it.

"We'll go with you, won't we Hilary?" said Gordon.

"Sure," said Hilary.

After they got permission from Ms. Foster, we started down the hall toward the library. "So what do you think about this Student Council stuff?" I asked carefully.

Hilary shrugged. "They do some cool things, but I wouldn't want to be on the council."

That surprised me. "Why not?" I thought *everyone* would want to be class representative.

"You have to miss class time to go to the meetings. I have a hard enough time getting homework done. I don't want to have to make up in-class stuff, too. Besides, I hate meetings." Hilary made a face. "It'd be like doing a group project. Everyone always has different ideas about what they should do and no one can agree, so they just end up arguing."

Getting out of class once in a while

didn't sound so bad to me. And I *like* group projects. When kids argue, I just tell a few jokes and get them laughing. It's hard to argue when you're in a good mood. "How about you?" I asked Gordon. "Don't you want to be the representative? You'd be good at it, you're so smart."

Gordon smiled. "Intelligence is one qualification, of course." He didn't say what he thought the other "qualifications" might be because by then we'd arrived at the library.

I showed our pass to Ms. Gardner, the librarian. Then Hilary said she was going to look for a collection of comics, and Gordon said he wanted to browse through the astronomy section. He got a telescope not long ago, and ever since then he's been crazy about the solar system and galaxies, and stuff like that. I was glad he and Hilary weren't going to follow me around because, like I said, I didn't want them to know my plan just yet.

While Hilary and Gordon were busy in different parts of the library, I asked Ms. Gardner for help finding a book that would teach me another language.

"I've got something better," she said, leading me to a bookshelf at the front of the room. She pointed to some plastic boxes. "These are cassette tape sets. You'll be able to *hear* the language instead of just seeing the words. That way you can learn correct pronunciation." She cocked her head. "I've got tapes for French and for Spanish. What language did you want to learn?"

I chose French, of course. I hoped it would sound as cool as Spanish. I also checked out the tallest, widest book I could find — it happened to be a book about whales — and laid it on top of the box of

tapes to hide them from Hilary and Gordon. As it turned out, I didn't need to bother. Gordon had his nose in a book on black holes all the way back to class, and Hilary kept reading me funny lines from her comic book.

4
"Coma Top L Too"

When I got home from school that afternoon Angie handed me a piece of paper as soon as I walked in the door. "I can write!" she said. I looked at the paper. The letters were big and wobbly, and the words kind of ran together, but I could read them. "I like the rain," I read aloud. "It makes big puddles. I put on my boots and splash around." I gulped. "Around" was one of the words

I'd missed on my spelling test that morning. *Aww, man.* Angie was already a better speller than me!

"Mommy helped," Angie said. "I told her the words, and she said what letters to put down."

Phew. Angie wasn't a better speller after all. "Nice story." I handed the paper back to her.

She followed me into my room. "Can I play with your Legos?" she asked as I shrugged off my backpack.

"Maybe later." I wanted to start on my French tapes. "Right now I need to study."

"I won't make any noise," Angie begged.

I rolled my eyes. It was impossible for Angie *not* to make noise. "Tell you what," I said. "I'll give you some Legos, and you can play in your own room. All right?"

Angie nodded. "Okay." She had some Legos of her own, but they were bigger ones, and she liked to play with my small ones. I wasn't sure if it was because of their smaller size, or because she just liked to play with my stuff. Mom says she doesn't let Angie play in my room when I'm away at school, but sometimes I find things in places I know I didn't leave them. I think she sneaks into my room when Mom isn't looking. But I don't have a lock on my door, so what can I do? At least she's never broken anything.

I found a shoe box in my closet and filled it with Legos. "Here you go," I said.

"Thanks." Angie took the box and hurried out of my room.

I closed my door. Then I fished the set of tapes out of my backpack. I loaded the first tape into my cassette recorder and pushed the PLAY button. "Bone sure," said a lady's voice. At least that's what it sounded like to me. "Welcome to 'Fun with French.'"

I settled back on my bed to listen.

"Repeat after me," said the lady. *"Bonjour."*

"Bone sure," I said. This wasn't so hard.

"You've just said, 'Hello,'" said the speaker. *I had?* "Now try this: *Bonjour. Je m'appelle Rachel. Comment t'appelles-tu?"*

Huh? What the heck was she saying now? I rewound the tape and listened again. The last part sounded like "coma top L too." But when I repeated what I thought she'd said I knew I hadn't said it quite right. I tried again.

Now the lady on the tape started singing a song about the "coma top L too." When she finished the song, she said, "Hello. My name is Rachel. What's your name?"

So that's what all that stuff she'd been saying meant!

I listened to and repeated a bunch more things. At the end of the tape, a boy and a girl had a whole conversation in French using the words I'd just practiced. They talked so fast I couldn't understand what they were saying even though I'd just practiced those very same words. I sighed. Learning French was going to be harder than I thought.

The phone rang. "I'll get it!" I heard Brock yell. His room is right next door to mine. A minute later, there was a knock on my door. I opened it. "Phone's for you," Brock said. He handed it to me.

"Hello?" I said.

"Hi," said Hilary. "Gordon's coming over in a few minutes. You want to come, too?"

I decided I needed a break. I could listen to more tapes later on. "Sure. I'll come."

“Great,” said Hilary. “I’ve got a new video game we can play.”

I left the tapes and my tape recorder on my bed and went to find Mom to tell her I was going over to Hilary’s.

“Come see what I made!” Angie yelled as I passed by her room.

I stuck my head in her door. Little groups of snapped together Legos covered her floor.

“It’s a playground,” Angie explained. She pointed to one group after another. “Here’s a slide. There’s the teeter-totter. That one’s the sandbox. And that’s the merry-go-round.”

When she pointed them out, I could really see what they were. Most kids her age would probably build something simple, like a tower. But not Angie. I gave her a thumbs-up. “Good job.”

Angie smiled and went back to work.

I found Mom in her office, sitting at her computer. I told her where I was going. "Be back for dinner at five-thirty," she said.

Hilary's house is about a ten-minute bike ride away. Gordon was already there when I arrived. "What do you get when you cross a chicken with an alien?" he asked when I walked in the door.

"You," I said.

Hilary laughed.

Gordon sniffed. "The correct answer is an eggs-traterrestrial."

I punched him in the shoulder. "Great joke."

Gordon raised an eyebrow. "You don't really think so."

"You tell him, Hilary," I said. "I always tell the truth, don't I?"

Hilary snorted. "There's an easy way to

tell when Josh is lying, Gordon — his lips move."

She and Gordon both laughed. "I didn't come here to be insulted," I said. Then I shrugged. "I usually go somewhere else for that."

"You'd make a good comedian," Gordon said later as we were playing Car Crazy, Hilary's new video game. "Or else a politician."

I glanced up from my game control, and the race car I was driving swerved. I steered it back onto the road. "A politician? Like the president, you mean?"

"Certainly," said Gordon as his blue car shot ahead of my red one. "Being funny is a plus in both jobs. Besides, you're good with people. They like you. Isn't that right, Hilary?" he said.

"President Josh Taylor," I said dreamily. "I kind of like that."

Hilary rolled her eyes. "You're going to give him a big head," she said as her yellow car flashed past both my car and Gordon's to cross the finish line.

"I could use a bigger head," I said, setting down my control. "Might make my ears look smaller."

Hilary laughed, but Gordon looked serious. "Have you thought about this Thursday's election for class representative?"

"A little," I admitted. Then I gulped. Gordon must be asking because *he* was interested in the job! Well if he was, then of course I'd vote for him.

My mouth fell open when he said, "I think you ought to run for the position."

"Me?" I said. "But what about you? Don't *you* want to be representative?"

"I've thought about it," said Gordon. "But I don't think I could get enough votes."

"Oh," I said, feeling kind of bad for him. Most of the kids in our class like Gordon better since Hilary and I helped him become less of a know-it-all, but he'll probably never be Mr. Popular. Not that *I* am. But I guess I do get along with most people.

Hilary turned off the TV. "Gordon and I could help you get elected, couldn't we, Gordon?"

"Certainly," said Gordon. "We could be your campaign managers."

"My *what-agers*?" I asked.

"Campaign managers. We'll plan ways to help you win the election."

"Like making VOTE FOR JOSH posters," Hilary said. "Stuff like that."

She and Gordon exchanged smiles, and suddenly I was suspicious.

"Hey," I said. "You two had this planned *before* I came over, didn't you?"

Hilary shrugged. "We talked about it on the way home from school a little. But so what? You *do* want to be class representative, don't you?"

"I guess so," I said, even though *more than anything* would've been a more truthful answer.

"Then it's settled," Gordon said, rubbing his hands together. "Tomorrow we'll nominate you for the job, and then we'll plan your campaign. With our eggs-pert assistance, you're sure to win!"

5
The Mystery of the Missing Recorder

As I pedaled home for dinner, I thought about what great friends I had. *Josh Taylor, Class Representative* sounded almost as good as *Josh Taylor, President.* After dinner I watched TV, until I remembered about my French tapes. I really didn't feel like listening some more, but I knew I'd better, or I'd never learn to speak French.

I dragged myself away from the TV, but when I got to my room my cassette recorder was missing! I was sure I'd left it sitting on my bed, but it wasn't there now.

"Hey," I yelled down the hall. "Did someone borrow my tape recorder?"

Brock poked his head out of his room. Holding up the phone, he scowled. "Quiet, please. I'm trying to have a conversation here."

"Sorry," I whispered. "Have you seen my recorder?"

Brock shook his head "no." Then he and the phone disappeared into his room again.

I stood looking at his closed door a few seconds. Brock needed to have a phone permanently inserted between his ear and his mouth, I thought. I wondered if someone had invented such a thing yet.

"Bonjour," said a voice at my elbow. I jumped. Somehow Angie had managed to sneak up next to me without my noticing. She held my cassette recorder out to me. *"Je m'appelle,* Angie," she jabbered. *"Comment t'appelles-tu?"*

I took the recorder, frowning. "Have you been listening to my tapes?" It was a dumb question.

Angie grinned. Then she started to sing the "Coma Top L Too" song. She must've listened to the whole first tape! Not only that. She sang the words *exactly* like the lady on the tape.

My stomach sunk. Learning French had been a *stupid* idea. Angie might be precocious, like Mom and Dad said, but she was also five years younger than me. It wasn't fair! I glared at her. "You know you're not supposed to go into my room without my permission," I scolded. "How would you like it if I came into *your* room and took *your* things?"

Angie's lower lip began to tremble, but I didn't stop. "You're a bad girl!" I yelled, shaking the recorder. "A very bad girl!" As soon as the words were out of my mouth, I knew I'd gone too far. Bursting into tears, Angie ran down the hall to her room.

I followed. Throwing herself onto her bed, Angie buried her face in her pillow. Her shoulders shook with sobs. I gulped. And Gordon had said I was "good with people." Ha!

I crouched next to Angie. "I'm sorry," I said softly. "I shouldn't have yelled at you like that. It was a mean thing to do."

Angie raised her tear-streaked face from

the pillow. She frowned. "I'm a . . . a . . . bad . . . girl," she stuttered.

"No, you're not. I just said that because I was mad. But I'm not mad anymore." I made myself smile. "See?"

Angie sat up. She pointed to the recorder still clutched in my hand. "Can I have it back?"

I sighed. "Don't you have your own?"

"It broke."

I laid the recorder on top of her bed. "Keep it as long as you want. I won't be using it after all."

Angie squealed. "Goody!"

I rolled my eyes. "You want the tapes, too?"

Angie nodded. "Thanks."

As I went back to my room, I wondered how Gordon and Hilary could think that I,

Mr. Average, would make a good class representative. Even my four-year-old sister was smarter than me. Why did I have to be such a loser? Maybe Gordon and Hilary had only suggested I run for class representative because they felt sorry for me.

6
Making Music

All Wednesday morning, I waited for Ms. Foster to talk about tomorrow's election. Finally, just after lunch recess as we lined up to go to music, she told us we'd discuss the election when we returned to class. I could hardly wait. Even if Hilary and Gordon only wanted to help me win because they felt sorry for me, that was okay. I'd still let them help. But I'd also try my hardest to become the best at something so that they wouldn't *have* to feel sorry for me — in case I didn't win.

About halfway through music, two older kids came into the room carrying instrument cases. When we'd finished the song we were singing, Mrs. Marshall, the music teacher, introduced them. "Carrie and John are going to accompany us on 'A Gift to Be Simple' during the choir assembly next week," she said. "They've come to practice with us."

As Mrs. Marshall was saying this, Carrie unlatched her case and took out a violin, while John put together a silver flute. While we waited, Mrs. Marshall ran across the room to a forest of black-painted music stands. She dragged two of them back, took some sheets of music from a folder, and placed the music on the stands. Carrie and John stepped up to play.

Mrs. Marshall waved her baton and started them off. Tapping their feet to the music, Carrie and John played a long sweep of notes that seemed to dance in the air. We were all so interested in watching and listening that when Mrs. Marshall motioned for the class to start singing, no one did. "Aren't they good?" I heard Hilary whisper. It was the same thing I was thinking.

Mrs. Marshall tapped her baton to get our attention. "When you're fifth graders," she told us, "you'll be able to take band or orchestra and learn to play an instrument, too." She smiled. "Shall we take it from the top again? This time be sure to watch me."

Later, as we were walking back to class, I couldn't stop thinking about how great it would be to play an instrument as well as Carrie and John. Maybe I could start now, instead of waiting till fifth grade. In Dad's office closet at home there used to be a trumpet — Dad played it in high school. Probably the trumpet was still there. Brock had never been interested in learning to play an instrument. Too busy with swimming.

The more I thought about learning to play Dad's trumpet, the better the idea sounded. And fortunately, Angie was too small to play an instrument. At least, I hoped she was.

If I couldn't be best at French, maybe I could be best at playing trumpet. And after I learned, I'd invite Hilary and Gordon over and play a concert just for them. They'd be so impressed they'd probably want me to play for the whole school.

Maybe they'd convince Dr. Wentworth, the principal, to let me play in the auditorium. They might even print up tickets and hand out programs at the door. Maybe they'd even call a TV reporter, who would film me and put me on the news.

My daydream was interrupted as we entered the classroom. After everyone sat down at their desks, Ms. Foster stood up at the front of the room. She ran a hand through her hair. As usual, it stuck out in all directions. "It's time now to decide who will run in our election for class representative tomorrow," she said.

Gordon jumped up from his desk. "I nominate Josh Taylor," he said.

"I second it," yelled Hilary.

Ms. Foster smiled. "Thank you, Gordon and Hilary. But we're not quite ready for nominations yet."

A few kids laughed.

Red-faced, Gordon and Hilary sat down. I squirmed in my chair.

Ms. Foster continued. "I want you to think carefully before you nominate someone. This is not a popularity contest." She paused. "Don't nominate your best friend unless you think they're really the best person for this job."

My face grew warm. I wondered if she'd been thinking of Gordon and Hilary and me when she said that.

Nicola Guest, who sits in the row ahead of me, raised her hand. "Can you nominate yourself?" she asked.

"If you think you would do the best job," said Ms. Foster. She glanced around the classroom. "All right then. Let's get started. Please raise your hand to nominate someone. I'll write the names of those nominated on the board."

In the end, there were three names on the board: mine, Carl's, and Nicola's. Nicola

MUSIC
CLASS
TODAY

didn't have to nominate herself after all, because her friend Stephanie did it, and Alicia seconded the nomination. There were a couple of others who were nominated, too, but they said they didn't want to be class representative, so Ms. Foster didn't put their names on the board.

"Can we make posters and give out buttons and things tomorrow to ask other people to vote for us?" Nicola asked as we were getting ready to go home at the end of the day.

Ms. Foster was silent for a moment. "Yes, I think that would be all right," she said at last. "But I don't want anyone spending a lot of money on that kind of stuff." She paused. "How about if we agree that no candidate can spend more than five dollars on their campaign?" She paused. "And that would include your friends' money as well as your own. Five dollars total."

We all agreed that that was fair, and I was glad because I'd spent most of my saved allowance on Legos and only had a few dollars left. I didn't want Hilary and Gordon to spend any of their money on me.

When the bell rang, I walked part of the way home with Hilary and Gordon. "How about if we meet at your house after dinner to make posters and plan your campaign?" Gordon asked.

"Okay," I said. I thought we had paper at home for posters. At least I hoped so. Then I wouldn't have to buy any.

"I'll bring a bunch of markers to color with," said Hilary.

We agreed to meet at seven, then I split off from the two of them since I live in a different direction.

7
Trumpets and Posters

When I arrived home, Brock was sitting at the kitchen table with his ear to the phone, as usual.

"Where is everyone?" I asked as I helped myself to the last granola bar in the box. The house was too quiet for Angie to be home, and I hadn't seen Mom or Dad, either.

"Hold on a second, Alan." Frowning, Brock covered the phone with his hand. "It's impossible to have an uninterrupted conversation in this house," he complained. "Mom and Dad and Angie went grocery shopping. They'll be back in an hour or so." He and the phone moved into the living room.

Aww, man. He didn't have to be such a grouch all the time. He was *always* on the phone. How else could I talk to him except by interrupting?

I finished the granola bar and poured myself a glass of milk. Then Brock came back into the kitchen. He set the phone down. "I'm going to the park to play basketball with some other guys," he said. "Tell Mom and Dad I'll be back in time for dinner, okay?"

I nodded. "See you."

Brock grunted. His way of saying "good-bye."

I drained my glass and set it in the sink.

Then remembering my earlier plan, I decided to look in Dad's office to see if his trumpet was still in the closet. I slid the doors open. Several cardboard boxes were stacked on the floor of the closet. I dragged them out, and behind one stack was a dusty brown instrument case. I wiped off the dust. Then I opened the case and lifted out the trumpet. Fitting the mouthpiece onto the trumpet, I brought it up to my mouth.

I took a deep breath and blew as hard as I could. Air rushed out, but no music. I puffed up my cheeks like a chipmunk, and blew again. Nothing. I tried pressing up and down on the button-things on top of the trumpet while I blew, but still nothing happened. Except my face got hot, and I started to feel dizzy.

I decided I needed some fresh air. Dad's office has a sliding glass door leading to the backyard. I slid the door open and stepped outside with the trumpet tucked under my arm. After taking a few big gulps of air, I put the trumpet up to my lips and tried blowing again. Not a sound. Out of the corner of my eye, I noticed the neighbor's fat gray cat creeping along the fence toward this maple tree in our backyard. A bird feeder hangs from the tree, and the cat was heading right for it.

"Scat!" I shouted. But the cat just ignored me. Pursing my lips, I blew on the trumpet so hard my eyes almost popped out. A weird, groaning noise that sounded like a wounded buffalo came out the end of the trumpet. The cat dashed down the fence and disappeared into its own backyard.

I grinned. If I couldn't make *music* with the trumpet, at least I'd found another use for it. But maybe I'd wait till fifth grade to

learn to play it properly. It might be easier by then.

Returning the trumpet to its case, I buried it in the back of Dad's closet again. Then I began restacking the cardboard boxes. One of the boxes was really heavy, and I dropped it when I tried to lift it. The box fell sideways, and books spilled out onto the carpet. Probably books my dad had owned when he was a kid; they looked pretty old. I tossed them back in the box till I came across one whose title caught my eye: *Card Trick Magic.*

Hmm. I thumbed through the book. The directions for each trick included lots of pictures and diagrams that didn't look too hard to follow. Maybe I could learn a few tricks. I could perform them for Hilary and Gordon since my concert idea had fizzled.

* * *

Hilary and Gordon arrived together at seven. Hilary had brought markers, and Mom found some white construction paper in a cupboard in the family room. We tried to think of things to write on the posters.

Hilary waved a blue marker in the air. "An idea just went through my head."

"That's because there's nothing to stop it," I said.

"Ha-ha," said Hilary. "How's this: 'Vote for Josh, by gosh.'"

"Sounds good," I said.

"How about this one?" said Gordon. "Don't be a squash, vote for Josh."

Hilary and I rolled our eyes.

Gordon shrugged. "There aren't a lot of words that rhyme with Josh."

We ended up making three posters using Hilary's idea, and two more that just said

VOTE FOR JOSH FOR CLASS REPRESENTATIVE. After we finished the last poster, I figured we were ready for tomorrow, but Gordon said, "We need something besides posters."

"Like what?" I said.

"I bet Nicola will hand out buttons," said Hilary. "I heard her tell Stephanie her mom had a button machine."

Gordon nodded. "Eggs-actly. That's why we need some kind of gimmick."

"A *what-tick*?" I asked.

"A gimmick," Gordon repeated. "Something that will get everybody to notice you."

Hilary snapped her fingers. "Josh could wear a costume!"

"No way," I said, thinking of the fluffy bunny suit I wore last Halloween because Mom had gotten it cheap at a garage sale. She'd been so excited about her "find" that I didn't have the heart to tell her I didn't want to wear it. Fortunately, my jacket covered most of it.

"We could have a parade out on the playground," Hilary went on. "You could carry a VOTE FOR JOSH sign, Gordon. I could wear my Wonder Woman costume and turn cartwheels or something. We could buy a bag of candy, and Josh could throw pieces to the crowd."

Gordon frowned. "There must be simpler ways to attract attention. And since we want everyone's attention focused on Josh, maybe it should be something only he does?"

A lightbulb went on in my head. "I could do a card trick!"

8
Josh Taylor, Magician

The next morning at school I patted the deck of cards in my pants pocket as I hung up my jacket. Last night I'd showed Hilary and Gordon *Card Trick Magic*, and they'd helped me choose a trick. I practiced it on them several times, until I could perform it without even thinking about it.

I could hardly wait to show everyone else the trick. They were going to be so amazed!

Maybe I'd learn more tricks after today. I could become an expert at card tricks. Instead of *Mr. Average*, I'd be *Josh Taylor, Magician*. And with luck, after tomorrow, *Josh Taylor, Class Representative*, too.

On my way to my desk I spotted Hilary at the pencil sharpener at the side of the room. Her back was to me as I sneaked up behind her. She was humming a song that sounded kind of familiar. It could've been one of the songs we practiced in music yesterday, but the way Hilary was humming it, it was hard to say. She couldn't carry a tune if it had a *handle*.

I tapped her on the back. "I love music," I said. "But please, keep on humming anyway."

Hilary jumped about a foot in the air. "I wish you wouldn't sneak up on me like that."

I grinned. "I brought my cards," I said, patting the deck in my pocket again.

"Great," Hilary said. "I asked Ms. Foster, and she said she'll let everyone put up their posters and do their campaign stuff after our math time tests this morning."

The bell rang, and we both hurried off to our desks.

A few minutes later, Gordon came by with the time tests. "You can keep mine," I said when Gordon handed me my test. "I've decided to be absent today."

Gordon grinned. "*Tsk, tsk.* How will you perform your card trick if you're absent?"

"Oh, all right," I said, pretending to grumble. "I'll take the test."

Being Mr. Average, I was on Level E on the time tests, the level most of the class was on. Gordon was probably on Level Z by now, if the levels went up that high. I would never be as good at math as him.

After the time test, which I hoped I'd passed, I needed to use the bathroom. On the way back to class I stopped at the drinking fountain in the hall. Carl and Mark were already there. I wondered if Carl wanted to win the election as badly as I did. I wanted to ask if he'd had as much trouble as Hilary and Gordon and I did coming up with stuff to write on our posters, but Carl kept slurping and slurping.

"Hurry up," said Mark. "I've counted to ten twice. Your turn is up."

One of our class rules is that we're not supposed to drink for longer than ten seconds when there's a line at the fountain.

Carl stopped drinking to glare at Mark. "You count too fast." He bent over the fountain again.

Mark shoved him in the back.

"Hey!" Carl spun around. Water dripped off his face. "Look what you did!" he yelled, pushing Mark back.

Mark clenched his hands into fists.

Uh-oh, I thought, *here comes a fight.* "Hey, guess what?" I said quickly. "My grandpa has a dog that can play chess."

"Huh?" said Carl.

Mark raised an eyebrow. "I've never heard of a dog that could do that. He must be really smart."

I smiled. "Not really. My grandpa usually wins."

Carl groaned.

"Oh," said Mark a few seconds later. "I get it." His fists unclenched.

Phew. "My grandpa really loves that dog," I said as Mark took his turn at the fountain. "He takes him everywhere. Once he even

took him to the shopping mall. Only dogs weren't allowed inside." I paused. "Grandpa had to leave him in the barking lot."

After my turn at the fountain, Carl, Mark and I walked back to the room together. Kids had already started putting up posters.

"Shoot!" said Carl. "I forgot about the posters." He hurried off to his desk.

Hilary came up and handed me one of the posters we'd made last night. She also gave me a long strip of tape.

"Why don't you put it up over there?" she said, pointing to the back of the room at a space above the coat racks.

As I went to put up the poster I passed Carl's desk. He was ripping a wad of paper out of a spiral notebook. I hesitated. "Do you need help?" I asked.

"No, I'm fine," he said. "This won't take

long." He grabbed a black marker from inside his desk, and scribbled "Vote for Carl" on the top sheet of paper.

I thought the posters Hilary, Gordon and I had made looked pretty good, but then I saw Nicola's posters. She and Stephanie had used pieces of cloth, glitter paint, buttons, and marker on big sheets of tagboard to spell out things like NICOLA GUEST, SHE'S THE BEST, and VOTE FOR GUEST. SHE'S BETTER THAN THE REST.

Hilary must've seen me staring at Nicola's posters. She came up to me at the coat racks. "Here's what I think her posters should say," she whispered: "NICOLA GUEST. SHE'S A PEST."

I couldn't help smiling. But really, Nicola's posters looked a lot better than ours. I crossed my fingers that my card trick would help our campaign. It was nearly time to perform it.

9
The Trick

"Ladies and gentlemen," Gordon called out when only a few minutes remained until recess. "May I have your attention, please."

Everyone, including Ms. Foster, looked at him. She knew what was going on, though, because Gordon told me he'd asked permission before passing out the math tests this morning.

I fingered the cards in my pocket. *This was it!*

"A good class representative should understand others well," Gordon said. "Josh Taylor not only *understands* others, some might say he can actually read minds!"

That was my cue. Pulling the deck of cards from my pocket, I stepped up to the front of the room. Automatically, everyone moved to sit on the floor near my feet. "To demonstrate my mind-reading skills, I will need a volunteer," I said.

Several kids waved their hands in the air. I wanted to pick Hilary, but she and Gordon and I had decided I shouldn't, because then kids might think she was in on the trick — that we were cheating.

"Alicia," I said. It was a safe choice; she was friends with Stephanie and Nicola.

Alicia came up to stand beside me. Holding the deck in my right hand, just like I'd practiced at home, I flicked through the cards with my thumb, separating them. "Please tell me which card you want me to stop at," I said to Alicia.

"Oh," said Carl. "I get it."

"You do?" I asked, disappointed. Carl was smart, but I'd hoped no one would be able to figure the trick out — at least not *quite* so fast.

"Sure," said Carl. "You're going to show us a card trick."

Phew. That's all he'd meant.

"There," Alicia said, stopping me about two-thirds of the way through the deck.

Using my left hand, I opened the deck like a book at the point where she'd told me to stop.

Everyone scooted in closer to see. It made

me a little nervous having so many kids watch. I tried to remember the next step.

"Okay, Alicia," I said, holding out the lower third of the deck. "Now take the card on top, the one you chose, and memorize it. Then put it back in the deck."

She did.

I handed the deck to Carl. "I want you to shuffle these really well."

Carl shuffled the cards several times, then handed them back to me. Making a big show of it, I threw them in the air.

A roar went up as the cards scattered all over the carpet.

"Hmpf," said Nicola. "Now I suppose we get to help you pick them up."

"Not at all," I said, pouncing on a card that had landed face up.

I showed the card to the audience. "The

eight of clubs, ladies and gentlemen!" I waved the card under Alicia's nose.

"Actually," said Alicia, sounding sorry, "that's not the right card."

Everyone burst out laughing. Everyone but Hilary, Gordon and me, that is.

My face grew warm. I'd practiced this trick dozens of times. Why hadn't it worked this time?

Feeling desperate, I picked up another card. "Is this the one?"

Alicia shook her head no.

"How about this one?" I said, picking up another card.

"I see how this works," Carl joked. "You just keep showing her cards until you get the right one."

Everyone cracked up again.

Ms. Foster clapped her hands together. "Okay, everyone. That's enough."

I bent down quietly and started picking up the cards.

Hilary and Gordon helped. In a kind voice, Ms. Foster said, "Want to try again? I bet it would work the second time."

I shook my head no. I sure as heck didn't want to mess up twice.

By now everyone was picking up cards. They probably felt sorry for me. Why did everything I do turn out so badly? Learning to play the trumpet had been a disaster, too. Except for scaring the neighbor's cat.

And Angie was still listening to the set of French tapes I'd brought home. While I was here at school she probably held whole *conversations* in French with her teddy bear and her dolls.

Sighing, I picked up another card. This trick should've been easy, but somehow I'd managed to mess it up, like everything else I did. The only thing I was really good at, besides wiggling my ears and telling a few jokes, was failure. How could I win the election now? I'd never be Number One at *anything*. Not even Number Two, Three, or Four. Heck. If anyone gave me a number right now it would have to be *Zero*. That's what I was, a big, fat Zero. And worse than that, I'd let my friends down.

10
Weekend Plans

When the recess bell rang, I wished I didn't have to go outside. I didn't want to talk to anyone. I couldn't face Hilary and Gordon right now and I wasn't sure they would want to talk to *me*, either.

Nicola and Stephanie were standing near the door. As everyone went outside, the two of them handed out red-white-and-blue VOTE

NICOLA
GUEST
VOTE FOR NICOLA
VOTE FOR NICOLA
VOTE FOR NICOLA

 buttons, and pieces of homemade fudge.

I was the last one out the door. "Good fudge," I said, taking a bite.

"Thanks," said Stephanie. "I made it."

"Too bad about your card trick," Nicola said, and she sounded like she really meant it. Somehow that only made me feel worse.

I spied Hilary and Gordon standing in line at the wall-ball court. When they looked in my direction, I ducked behind a tree at the side of the playground. I stayed there the whole recess.

After recess, I gave my cards away to Carl as we sat down at our desks. "Maybe you could use them in one of your science experiments," I told him. "Like if you need something to blow up."

"Gee, thanks," he said. "But are you

sure you don't want to keep them? You might want to learn other tricks."

I rolled my eyes. "I'd have more fun hitting my thumb with a hammer."

At lunchtime, Hilary cornered me at the coat racks when I went to get my lunch out of my backpack. "Where were you at recess?" she asked. "Gordon and I kept looking for you, but we never saw you."

I couldn't think what to say, so I just shrugged.

"Come eat lunch with Gordon and me," Hilary said.

Carrying my lunch bag, I followed her to Gordon's desk. Neither of them said anything about my failed card trick *or* the election. Instead, they talked about their plans for the weekend. We didn't have school tomorrow because it was a Teachers' Workshop Day. That meant that the teachers had to come to school, but not us. We'd be off for three whole days.

Hilary took a bite out of an apple. "My family's going to the beach for the weekend," she said after she'd swallowed. "We're leaving early tomorrow morning."

"Sounds like fun," said Gordon. He sprinkled salt on a hard-boiled egg. "I'm going to visit my grandparents. They live on a farm, and last time I visited they let me drive the tractor."

I poked at my bologna sandwich and said nothing. My family wasn't going anywhere this weekend. Brock had a swim meet on Saturday, and Angie had been invited to *two* birthday parties. *I* was the only one without any plans. It was just one more proof of my Zero-ness.

Gordon eyed my uneaten sandwich. "Aren't you hungry?" he asked.

I shook my head. “Do you want it?”

“Certainly.”

Gordon gobbles down leftovers like a vacuum cleaner sucking up dirt. I handed him my sandwich.

“I bet Nicola will win the election,” I said.

There was a pause. Hilary and Gordon looked at each other. Then Gordon said, “Guess where chickens wait to pay for their groceries?”

“Where?” asked Hilary.

“In the eggs-press line.”

“Argh,” said Hilary. “Your chicken jokes are getting worse.”

“I have another one,” said Gordon. “Or did I already tell it to you?”

“Was it funny?” asked Hilary.

“Yes.”

“Then you didn’t.”

I guess I didn't blame Gordon for changing the subject. He and Hilary probably figured Nicola would win the election, too, but they didn't want to say so. I wondered if *they'd* still vote for me.

11
The Vote

The day dragged on. After lunch recess, we had P.E. and then silent reading. Finally, it was social studies and time for the election.

Ms. Foster faced the class. "Before we vote, remember that a class representative represents the whole class, not just him or herself. Choose the person you feel will represent our class best and work well with representatives from all the other classes."

Hilary glanced back at me, and I saw several other kids looking at me, too. My face grew warm; they were probably remembering my doomed card trick.

Ms. Foster passed everyone a small blank piece of paper. "When you are ready, you may write down the name of the candidate you think would do the best job as our representative. I'll tally the results afterward and send our choice to the office to be announced at the end of the day."

"Can we vote for ourselves if we want to?" Nicola asked.

"If you think you would do the best job," said Ms. Foster.

I thought about this carefully, and about the other things Ms. Foster had said, and then I made my choice.

The afternoon moved on in slow motion. I tried not to glance at the clock above the blackboard, but I couldn't help it. Each time I looked, only a few more minutes had passed. I don't know why I was in such a hurry to hear the results of the vote since I was sure I wouldn't win. But at least the waiting would be over.

Art followed afternoon recess and then science. Ms. Foster talked about the difference between igneous and sedimentary rocks, but I had a hard time concentrating. It was like I had rocks in my *head*.

I glanced at the clock again. Fifteen more minutes till the end of the day. I slid down in my seat. Weren't they *ever* going to make that announcement?

Finally, the intercom crackled to life.

Ms. Foster clapped her hands. "Quiet, everyone."

My stomach jumped. *This was it*.

"I am pleased to announce the names of the students who have been chosen to represent their classes on this year's student council," said a voice I recognized as Dr. Wentworth's. There was a pause, then she went on. "The fifth-grade representatives are Jenny Lee, Ward Lynn, and Greg Uratsu."

Down the hall cheers were coming from the fifth-grade classrooms. I held my breath.

Fourth grade would be next. There would be three names just like for fifth grade because there were three fourth-grade classrooms. Third grade would be last, and there were four third-grade classrooms.

"The representatives for fourth grade," Dr. Wentworth announced, "are Emily Wand, Kim Kellogg, and Shane Warner." A cheer went up from the girls in our class because Kim is Stephanie's sister.

"Before I go on," said Dr. Wentworth, "I'd just like to say how impressed I was with the names of the students chosen as representatives. Representatives should be good students and good role models, and your choices reflect this."

I gulped. I'd only been to see Dr. Wentworth once this year, and that was when I was in trouble for practicing wall-ball in a place I shouldn't have been. My heart sank. I almost covered my ears to keep from hearing the rest of the announcement. But then I wouldn't know for sure who had won. Instead, I sat on my hands.

"Third-grade representatives are Sami Stendal, Brianna Campbell, John Claymore, and . . ."

I shut my eyes and gritted my teeth.

". . . Josh Taylor."

My eyes flew open. *Me? They'd chosen me?*

Everyone yelled and whistled and clapped. Carl reached over and punched me in the shoulder. "Nice going."

Ms. Foster smiled from the front of the room. "Congratulations, Josh."

12
Going Home

When the bell rang, Hilary and Gordon rushed over to my desk.

"Congratulations, Mister Representative." Gordon grabbed my hand and shook it. "I just knew you'd win."

"So did I," said Hilary. "Good going, Josh."

"Thanks."

"Next step — the White House," Gordon said.

I grinned.

Hilary pretended to glare at Gordon. "I warned you not to give him a big head. Next thing you know, he'll want to be king or something."

"Why not? One of my ancestors was a king," I said.

Gordon raised an eyebrow. "Really? Who?"

I thumped my chest. "King Kong."

Gordon snorted. "Now that you mention it, I can see the resemblance."

As we made our way to the back of the room to grab our jackets and backpacks, Alicia came up to us. "I'm glad you won, Josh," she said.

"Gee, thanks." She was okay, for a girl.

Someone came up behind me and thumped me in the back. I turned.

"Congratulations," Mark said. "You got my vote."

"Really? Thanks a lot," I said.

Mark grinned. "Got any more stories about your grandpa's dog?"

Hilary raised an eyebrow. She'd heard those stories before.

"No more right now," I said. "But maybe later."

"I really didn't think I'd win," I confessed to Hilary and Gordon as we grabbed our stuff and made our way out the door. "Especially after I messed up that card trick so bad." I paused. "I was even worried *you'd* change your minds about voting for me."

Hilary snorted. "What a dumb idea!"

"That's for sure," said Gordon. "You were always the best person for the job."

Coming from Gordon, that meant a lot.

"I wasn't going to admit this," I said on our walk home. "But *I* voted for me, too."

Hilary rolled her eyes. "Looks like we're the Josh Taylor Fan Club. Pretty soon you'll be taking a bow every time you look in a mirror."

I grinned. "I do that already."

After I split off from Hilary and Gordon, I couldn't wait to get home. I imagined what my family would say when I told them I'd won the election. My parents would be proud of me. Angie would probably say something in French like "Ooo la la!" And maybe, just maybe, Brock would put down the phone to congratulate me, too.

I crossed the street and headed for my house. Monday would be my very first day as class representative. Maybe I should give a speech. I'd have plenty of time to write one since my family wasn't going anywhere this weekend. I wouldn't make the speech too long though, that might bore everyone. And I'd put in some good jokes because everybody likes to laugh.

I climbed the steps to the front door. I already knew how my speech would end: "I am honored to be your representative," I'd say. "I look forward to sharing all our good ideas with the council and I promise to do my very best."

I turned the knob and pushed the door open. "Hey, everyone," I called out. "I'm home."

Three kids, one wacky friendship . . .
What will they think of next?

Find out in *Third-Grade Friends #3 Hilary's Super Secret*

The door creaked open, and footsteps came into the room. I crouched under the desk, barely breathing. My heart was beating so loud I was sure Mr. Stenson would hear it. What would he say if he found me? What would he do? If only I hadn't opened my big mouth and suggested this stupid plan. If Mr. Stenson caught me, I'd never be able to explain what I'd been up to.

"Do you see it?" asked Mr. Stenson.

"Not yet," said Josh. I could hear him moving around the room.

"I came back to get something off my desk," Mr. Stenson said. "You keep looking."

I gasped as footsteps came closer to my hiding place. Then the toes of a big pair of shoes appeared, just inches from where I crouched. I heard thumps over my head, as Mr. Stenson shuffled through the stuff on his desk. "Here's that note I was looking for!" Mr. Stenson's voice boomed, he was so close. "Did you find your jacket?" he asked Josh.

"Must've left it somewhere else," Josh mumbled.

"Well, let's go, then. I need to make a call from the office before the bell rings."

After I heard the door slam shut, I waited a few more seconds before crawling out from under the desk. Then I dashed over to the closet, grabbed the guitar case, and snuck out the door.

Josh was waiting for me. He'd doubled back as soon as he could. I don't know how we managed to sneak that big guitar down the hall together without being seen, but we did. We were almost to the classroom when we heard footsteps again.

"In here, Josh!" I hissed, ducking into the girls' restroom.

"No way, Hilary," Josh said, tugging on his end of the guitar case. "I'm not going in there!"

"Don't be stupid," I whispered as the steps came closer. "We've got to hide!" I pulled on my end of the guitar, and Josh came with it. . . .

About the Author

Suzanne Williams is horrible at card tricks, doesn't know how to play the trumpet, and has never been able to get the hang of pronouncing French words correctly. A former elementary school librarian, she is the author of several children's books including the Children's Choice Award–winning picture book, *Library Lil.*

Suzanne lives near Seattle, Washington with her husband, Mark, her daughter, Emily, and her son, Ward. You can visit Suzanne on the Web at *www.suzanne-williams.com.*